THIS WALKER BOOK BELONGS TO:

First published individually as *Five Minutes' Peace* (1986),
*All in One Piece* (1987), *A Piece of Cake* (1989) and
*A Quiet Night In* (1993) by Walker Books Ltd
87 Vauxhall Walk, London SE11 5HJ

This edition published 2004

2 4 6 8 10 9 7 5 3 1

© 1986, 1987, 1989, 1993 Jill Murphy

The right of Jill Murphy to be identified as author/illustrator
of this work has been asserted by her in accordance with the
Copyright, Designs and Patents Act 1988

This book has been typeset in Monotype Bembo

Printed in China

All rights reserved

British Library Cataloguing in Publication Data:
a catalogue record for this book is available from the British Library

ISBN 0-7445-8228-8

www.walkerbooks.co.uk

# THE LARGE FAMILY COLLECTION

## JILL MURPHY

Walker Books
AND SUBSIDIARIES
LONDON · BOSTON · SYDNEY · AUCKLAND

FOR EVIE

LAST BUT NOT LEAST ♥ WITH MUCH LOVE

# Five Minutes' Peace

The children were having breakfast.
This was not a pleasant sight.

Mrs Large took a tray from the
cupboard. She set it with a teapot,
a milk jug, her favourite cup and
saucer, a plate of marmalade toast
and a leftover cake from yesterday.
She stuffed the morning paper
into her pocket and sneaked off
towards the door.

9

"Where are you going with that tray, Mum?" asked Laura.

"To the bathroom," said Mrs Large.

"Why?" asked the other two children.

"Because I want five minutes' peace from *you* lot," said Mrs Large.

"That's why."

"Can *we* come?" asked Lester as they trailed up the stairs behind her.

"No," said Mrs Large, "you can't."

"What shall *we* do then?" asked Laura.

"You can play," said Mrs Large.

"Downstairs. By yourselves. And keep an eye on the baby."

"I'm *not* a baby," muttered the little one.

Mrs Large ran a deep, hot bath. She emptied half a bottle of bath-foam into the water, plonked on her bath-hat and got in. She poured herself a cup of tea and lay back with her eyes closed. It was heaven.

"Can I play you my tune?" asked Lester.

Mrs Large opened one eye. "Must you?" she asked.

"I've been practising," said Lester. "You told me to. *Can* I? Please, just for *one* minute."

"Go *on* then," sighed Mrs Large.

So Lester played. He played "Twinkle, Twinkle, Little Star" three and a half times.

12

In came Laura. "Can I read you a page from my reading book?" she asked.

"*No*, Laura," said Mrs Large. "Go on, *all* of you, off downstairs."

"You let Lester play his tune," said Laura. "I heard. You like him better than me. It's not fair."

"Oh, don't be silly, Laura," said Mrs Large. "Go *on* then. Just *one* page."

So Laura read. She read four and a half pages of "Little Red Riding Hood".

In came the little one with a trunkful of toys.

"For *you*!" he beamed, flinging them all into the bath water.

"Thank you, dear," said Mrs Large weakly.

"Can I see the cartoons in the paper?" asked Laura.

"Can I have the cake?" asked Lester.

"Can I get in with you?" asked the little one.

Mrs Large groaned.

In the end they all got in. The little one was in such a hurry that he forgot to take off his pyjamas.

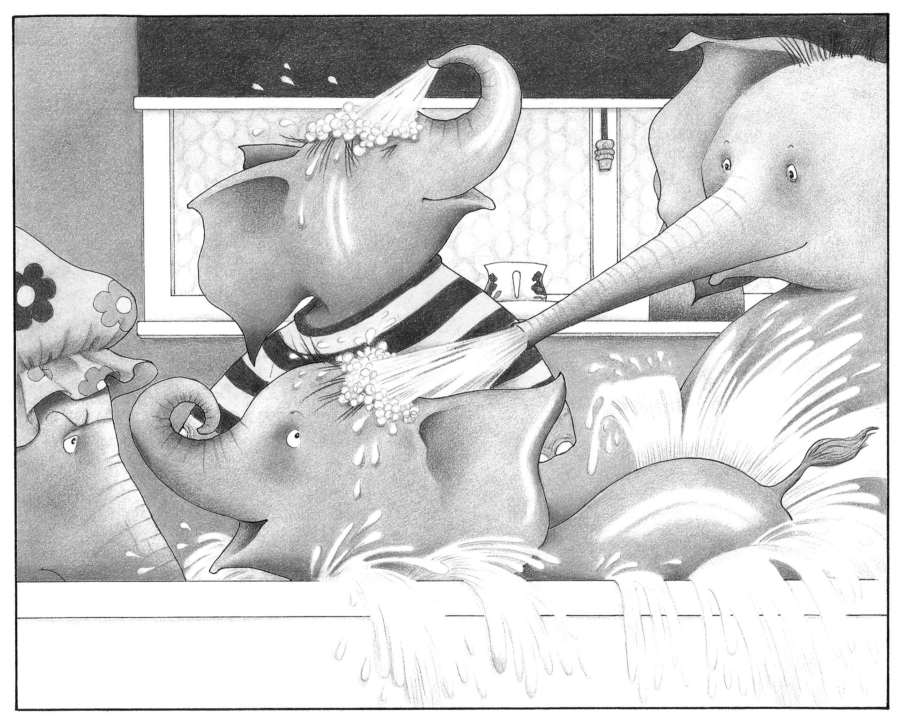

Mrs Large got out. She dried herself, put on her dressing-gown and headed for the door.

"Where are you going now, Mum?" asked Laura.

"To the kitchen," said Mrs Large.

"Why?" asked Lester.

"Because I want five minutes' peace from *you* lot," said Mrs Large. "That's why."

And off she went downstairs, where she had three minutes and forty-five seconds of peace…

19

...before they all came to join her.

# All in One Piece

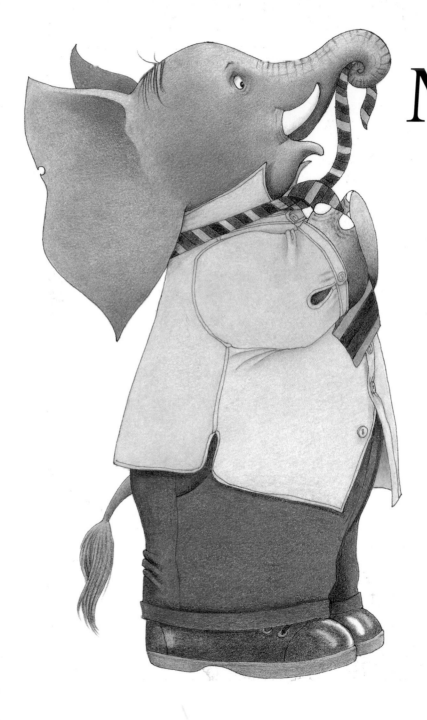

Mr Large was getting ready for work. "Don't forget the office dinner-dance tonight, dear," he said.

"Of course I won't," said Mrs Large. "I've been thinking about it all year."

"Are children allowed at the dinner-dance?" asked Lester.

"No," said Mrs Large. "It'll be too late for little ones."

"What about the baby?" asked Luke.

"Granny is coming to take care of everyone," said Mrs Large, "so there's no need to worry."

Granny arrived at tea time. The children were already bathed and in their nightclothes. Granny gave them some painting to do while she tidied up and Mr and Mrs Large went upstairs to get ready.

Luke sneaked into the bathroom while Mr Large was shaving. "Will I have to shave when I grow up?" he asked, patting foam onto his trunk.

"Go away," said Mr Large. "I don't want you ruining my best trousers!"

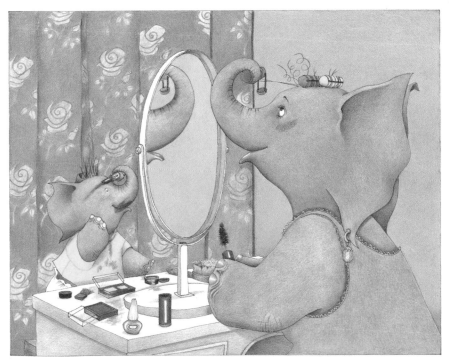

The baby crept into the bedroom where Mrs Large was putting on her make-up. Mrs Large didn't notice until it was too late.

"Look!" said the baby. "Pretty!"

"Don't move," said Mrs Large. "Don't touch *anything*!"

Outside on the landing, things were even worse. Laura was clopping about in her mother's best shoes and beads and Lester and Luke were seeing how many toys they could cram into her new tights.

"Downstairs at once!" bellowed Mrs Large. "Can't I have just one night in the whole year to myself? One night when I am not covered in jam and poster-paint? One night when I can put on my new dress and walk through the front door all in one piece?"

27

The children went downstairs to Granny. Mr Large
followed soon after, very smart in his best suit. At last,
Mrs Large appeared in the doorway.
"How do I look?" she asked.

"Pretty, Mummy!" gasped the children.

"What a smasher!" said Mr Large.

"You look like a film star, dear," said Granny.

"Hands off!" said Mrs Large to the paint-smeared children.

Mr and Mrs Large got ready to leave. "Goodbye everyone," they said. "Be good now."

The baby began to cry.

"Just go," said Granny, picking her up. "She'll stop as soon as you've left. Have a lovely time."

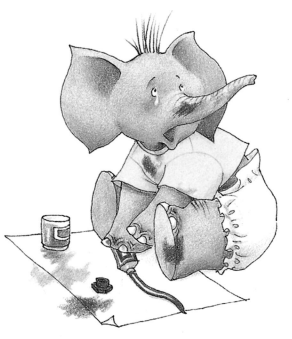

"We've escaped," said Mr Large with a smile, closing the front door
  behind them.

"All in one piece," said Mrs Large, "and not a smear of paint between us."

"Actually," said Mr Large gallantly, "you'd look wonderful to me,
  even if you were covered in paint."

Which was perfectly true …
and just as well really!

# A Piece of Cake

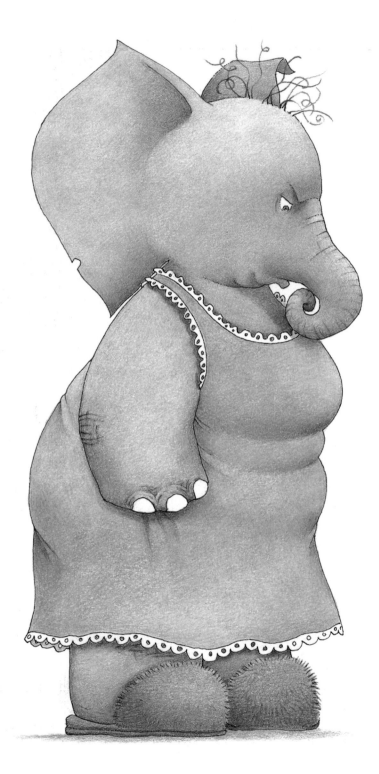

"I'm fat," said Mrs Large.
"No you're not," said Lester.
"You're our cuddly mummy,"
 said Laura.
"You're just right," said Luke.
"Mummy's got wobbly bits,"
 said the baby.
"Exactly," said Mrs Large.
"As I was saying – I'm fat.
 We must all go on a diet.
 No more cakes. No more
 biscuits. No more crisps.
 No more sitting around
 all day. From now on,
 it's healthy living."

"Can we watch TV?" asked Lester, as they trooped in from school.

"Certainly not!" said Mrs Large.

"We're all off for a nice healthy jog round the park."

And they were.

"What's for tea, Mum?" asked Laura when they arrived home.

"Some nice healthy watercress soup," said Mrs Large. "Followed by a nice healthy cup of water."

"Oh!" said Laura. "That sounds … nice."

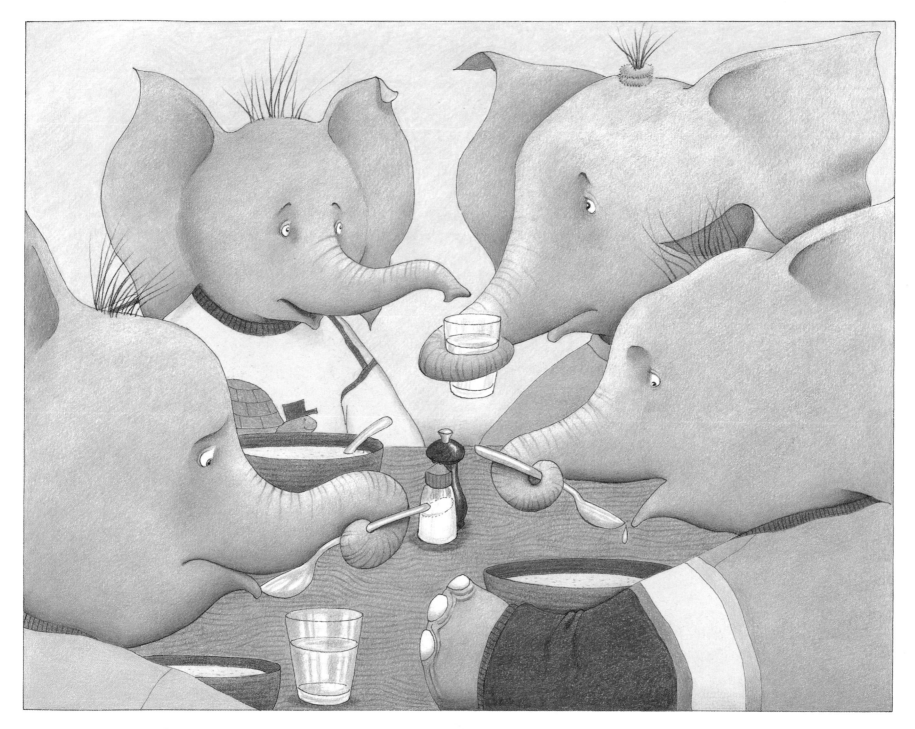

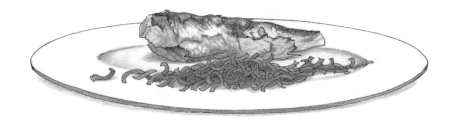

"I'm just going to watch the news, dear," said Mr Large when he
   came home from work.

"No you're not, dear," said Mrs Large.

"You're off for a nice healthy jog round the park, followed by your
   tea – a delicious sardine with grated carrot."

"I can't wait," said Mr Large.


It was awful. Every morning there was a healthy breakfast followed
by exercises. Then there was a healthy tea followed by a healthy jog.
By the time evening came everyone felt terrible.

41

"We aren't getting any thinner, dear," said Mr Large.

"Perhaps elephants are *meant* to be fat," said Luke.

"Nonsense!" said Mrs Large. "We mustn't give up now."

"Wibbly-wobbly, wibbly-wobbly," went the baby.

One morning a parcel arrived. It was a cake from Granny. Everyone stared at it hopefully. Mrs Large put it into the cupboard on a high shelf. "Just in case we have visitors," she said sternly.

Everyone kept thinking about the cake. They thought about it during tea. They thought about it during the healthy jog. They thought about it in bed that night.

Mrs Large sat up. "I can't stand it any more," she said to herself. "I must have a piece of that cake." Mrs Large crept out of bed and went downstairs to the kitchen. She took a knife out of the drawer and opened the cupboard. There was only one piece of cake left!

"Ah ha!" said Mr Large, seeing the knife. "Caught in the act!"
Mrs Large switched on the light and saw Mr Large and all the children hiding under the table.

"There *is* one piece left," said Laura in a helpful way.
Mrs Large began to laugh. "We're all as bad as each other!" she said, eating the last piece of cake before anyone else did.
"I do think elephants are meant to be fat," said Luke.
"I think you're probably right, dear," said Mrs Large.

"Wibbly-wobbly, wibbly-wobbly!"
went the baby.

# A Quiet Night In

50

I want you all in bed early tonight," said Mrs Large. "It's Daddy's birthday and we're going to have a quiet night in."

"Can we be there too?" asked Laura.

"No," said Mrs Large. "It wouldn't be quiet with you lot all charging about like a herd of elephants."

"But we *are* a herd of elephants," said Lester.

"Smartypants," said Mrs Large. "Come on now, coats on. It's time for school."

That evening, Mrs Large had the children bathed and in their pyjamas before they had even had their tea. They were all very cross.

"It's only half past four," said Lester.

"It's not even dark yet."

"It soon will be," said Mrs Large grimly.

After tea, the children set about making place cards and decorations for the dinner table. Then they all tidied up. Then Mrs Large tidied up again.

Mr Large arrived home looking very tired.

"We're all going to bed," said Lester.

"So you can be quiet," said Laura.

"Without us," said Luke.

"Shhhh," said the baby.

"Happy Birthday," said Mrs Large. "Come and see the table."

Mr Large sank heavily into the sofa. "It's lovely, dear," he said, "but do you think we could have our dinner on trays in front of the TV? I'm feeling a bit tired."

"Of course," said Mrs Large. "It's *your* birthday. You can have whatever you want."

"We'll help," said Luke. The children ran to the kitchen and brought two trays.

"I'll set them," said Mrs Large. "We don't want everything ending up on the floor."

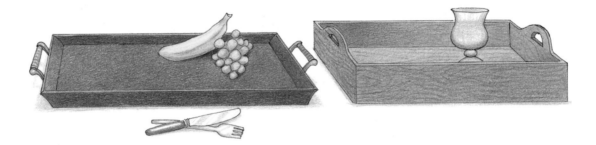

"Can we have a story before we go to bed?" asked Luke.

"Please," said Lester.

"Go on, Dad," said Laura. "Just one."

"Story!" said the baby.

"Oh, all right," said Mr Large. "Just one, then."

Lester chose a book and they all cuddled up on the sofa.

Mr Large opened the book and began to read: "One day Binky Bus drove out of the big garage. 'Hello!' he called to his friend, Micky Milkfloat – "

"I don't like that one," said Laura. "It's a boy's story."

"Look," said Mr Large, "if you're going to argue about it, you can all go straight to bed without *any* story."

So they sat and listened while Mr Large read to them.

After a while he stopped.

"Go on, Daddy," said Luke. "What happened after he bumped into Danny Dustcart?"

"Did they have a fight?" asked Lester.

"Look," said Laura. "Daddy's asleep."

"Shhhh!" said the baby.

Mrs Large laughed. "Poor Daddy," she said. "Never mind, we'll let him snooze a bit longer while I take you all up to bed."

"Will you just finish the story, Mum?" asked Lester.

"We don't know what happens in the end," said Luke.

"Please," said Laura.

"Story!" said the baby.

"Move up, then," said Mrs Large. She picked up the book and began to read: "'Watch where you're going, you silly Dustcart!' said Binky. Just then, Pip the Police Car came driving by…"

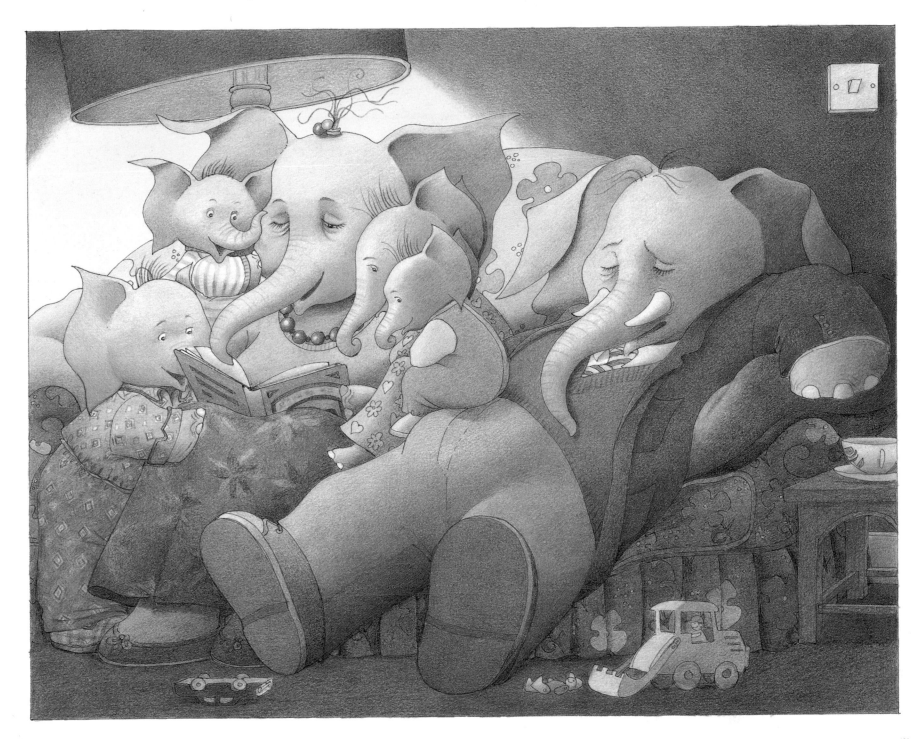

After a while, Mrs Large stopped reading.

"What's that strange noise?" asked Lester.

"It's Mummy snoring," said Luke. "Daddy's snoring too."

"They must be very tired," said Laura, kindly.

"Shhhh!" said the baby.

The children crept from the sofa and fetched a blanket. They covered Mr and Mrs Large and tucked them in.

"We'd better put ourselves to bed," said Lester. "Come on."

"Shall we take the food up with us?" asked Luke. "It *is* on trays."

"It's a pity to waste it," said Laura. "I'm sure they wouldn't mind. Anyway, they wanted a quiet night in."

"Shhhh!" said the baby.

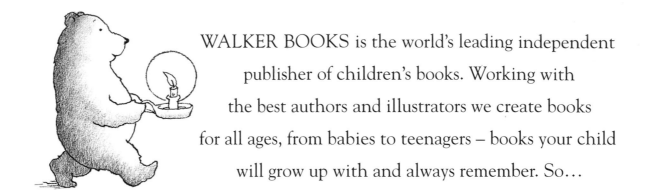

WALKER BOOKS is the world's leading independent
publisher of children's books. Working with
the best authors and illustrators we create books
for all ages, from babies to teenagers – books your child
will grow up with and always remember. So…

FOR THE BEST CHILDREN'S BOOKS, LOOK FOR THE BEAR